Illusion
of
Justice

M I K E   N A S H

Copyright © 2022 Mike Nash
All rights reserved
First Edition

PAGE PUBLISHING
Conneaut Lake, PA

First originally published by Page Publishing 2022

ISBN 978-1-6624-5652-7 (pbk)
ISBN 978-1-6624-5653-4 (digital)

Printed in the United States of America

CONTENTS

Chapter 1	The Journey Ahead	5
Chapter 2	Cultures Collide	8
Chapter 3	Tragedy Discovered	13
Chapter 4	Escape to the North	15
Chapter 5	Strength Returns	18
Chapter 6	A New Beginning—A New Life	21
Chapter 7	Life Gets Even Better	25
Chapter 8	Kearney Gets Tough	27
Chapter 9	A Real Family—A Real Home	33
Chapter 10	A Painful Loss Again	35
Chapter 11	Justice Comes Quickly	41
Chapter 12	Family by Choice	43
Chapter 13	A Family Bonded by Love	48
Chapter 14	Everything Changes	50
Chapter 15	Life Shattered Again	55
Chapter 16	The Illusion Begins	60
Chapter 17	Justice Prevails	66
Chapter 18	Hearts Begin to Heal	71
Chapter 19	Home for Summer	73

CHAPTER 1

The Journey Ahead

In the year 1873, going west by wagon train was coming to an end. The Continental Railroad had been completed and was much faster and safer but was also much more expensive for taking furniture, farm animals, and household goods. Jonas Clark, his wife Edna, his brother Owen, and their twin sons, James and Peter, had left Ohio and traveled to Independence, Missouri. They were to meet up with a guide and others in a small wagon train going west. The family were farmers and didn't know exactly where they were going, but felt they would know it when they saw it. Many stories had been told of the rich farmland in states to the west. The land was rich, and the weather was milder.

They arrived in Independence, Missouri, four days before the wagon train was scheduled to leave. This gave them time to meet the others and get everything well prepared for the long trip ahead. They had more animals than most—four mules, three cows, and the young dog, Albert. The wagon was a new Studebaker. It was not as big as some but was specially reinforced for additional strength to be able to endure any of the obstacles they would encounter on the journey. The wagon was equipped with two large water kegs, one on each side. They also had a toolbox, canvas, and a big trunk for clothes. The extra space was filled with some furniture, a sewing machine, various cooking utensils, and, of course, plenty of salt, flour, and coffee. Uncle Owen was only taking the bare necessities, but he did have an extra box. He had the box for a month, and wouldn't let anyone see what was inside of it. He would just say everyone would find out in due time, which of course, created more curiosity.

After supper, on the evening before leaving, Uncle Owen brought out the box and had James and Peter come sit with him. He opened the box and pulled out two of the new style, full-framed Army Colt 45 revolvers. Both had been nickeled and identically engraved. The grips were also identically carved from ivory. They had seven and a half inches barrels and were in matching custom tooled holsters. He showed them the only difference. On the butt of the grip was engraved their name. One had Peter, the other had James. They must have cost him a fortune.

Uncle Owen said, "These are for men and are tools that may be needed on the trip. Never be without them. If properly cared for, they can last a lifetime. I've had them specially tooled, and there are no other guns exactly the same as these. I also had the holsters specially made for these guns and tooled to match their beauty."

The boys were already proficient with their .36-caliber Navy percussion revolvers, but those revolvers were nothing like these new Colt 45s. The boys knew how special these guns were, and when thanking their uncle, they also promised to take care of them for their entire life. Uncle Owen knew a promise was a promise, and the boys would keep it. All Uncle Owen said was "I love you, and I am as proud of you as if you were my own two sons. I knew you would appreciate how special they are and have no doubt you will take care of them."

The following morning, twelve wagons pulled out just after dawn. It was early April, and the adventure was starting. You could sense the excitement in the air as the wagons lined up. Edna was driving the team of mules with the three cows pulled behind. She kept the wagon more toward the rear to see what problems the others were having. This way, a bad stream or rough trail was tested first with someone else's wagon. There was more dust, but the prewarning of a hazard made it worth it. The men all walked along beside the wagon close to the front. If there was any problem with the team, they could quickly respond. None were expected, as they had worked the mules together for several years. They were an exceptional team and worked well together. But it was still a good idea to keep close attention. The boys wore their Navy revolvers. The new Colts were kept in the wagon because they were too special for everyday carry.

The trail they were following had been used for several years and made for easy traveling. Most evenings, when they stopped to make camp, they were in meadows with plenty of grass for the animals and trees for shade. Every chance they had, they kept the water barrels filled. The trail was mostly rolling hills and no steep inclines. They had also found plenty of game to provide the travelers with meat. Each evening, after supper, people would get together and talk about their lives and their hopes for the future. The level of excitement remained high. Best of all, the weather seemed to cooperate. They had encountered some small rainstorms and light snow but, mostly at night, nothing to make travel difficult—just enough to keep the dust down and help maintain the water supply. The wagons were making about twelve to as much as fifteen miles a day. This was much better travel time than expected.

CHAPTER 2

Cultures Collide

By the end of the third week, the wagon train was getting close to Fort Kearny. Before stopping to make camp for the evening, they were met by a group of soldiers. There was an officer, six soldiers, and an Indian who seemed to be their guide. The wagons all pulled to a stop, and the people gathered around to talk with the soldiers. What they had to say was not good. The officer spoke to the wagon master and warned them to be on the alert because of an Indian problem. He said most of the conflict between the Indians and the Whites had been settled years before, and things had been peaceful. However, that peace had been shattered because of some cowboys a week earlier. The cowboys raided a small Indian hunting camp. Most of the younger men from the camp had been out hunting. The cowboys rode into the camp and killed several children, raped the younger women, and tortured the older men before killing them. When the hunting party returned to their camp, they were told by the survivors what had happened. They were not on their normal hunting grounds and couldn't give a proper tribal farewell to those killed. The best they could do was bury them similar to what the White man does. The survivors then split into two groups. One group went to what was left of Fort Kearny to report the incident. But the others, the hunting party and the rest of the survivors, about forty in all, left seeking revenge.

ILLUSION OF JUSTICE

The officer said they had already caught the cowboys and three had been killed while being captured. The other three were going to be tried. The officer said the Indians were not aware of their capture and had already raided two farms, killing four people and burning the buildings to the ground. The officer apologized for not being able to leave any men for protection and explained the Fort had officially been closed a couple of years ago. He said the men with him and the three left at the Fort were all that remained in the area. He then ordered his men to saddle up, and they rode off to the north to continue their search for the Indians.

Making camp that evening was done with much concern toward their safety. The wagons were grouped in a tighter circle, and the animals were all kept within the ring. However, there was also excitement knowing they were only about thirty miles from the old fort. Their guide had told them there is also a small town nearby called Dobytown. He explained it got its name because the buildings were made from adobe clay. Most of the people had left the town when the Army left Fort Kearny, but there were some farming families that had stayed behind and they always enjoyed greeting the wagons. The soldiers had told the guide the trail was in good condition and felt the wagons could probably make it there in two to three days. The guide had made the trip several times before, and he agreed.

The following morning was beautiful. People were already stirring by first light. Breakfast was quickly served, and the teams were being readied for the day ahead. Uncle Owen was outside the camp and came running in quickly between two of the wagons. He instantly got everyone's attention and pointed out to the horizon in several different directions. They could barely be seen, but in every direction he pointed, there were Indians. They had completely surrounded the wagon train during the night. Uncle Owen did his best to keep everyone calm and said he would walk out and try to talk to them. He raised his hands and made sure they could see him lay his rifle against a wagon and started walking toward the Indians that were the closest to the wagons. By the time he had gotten no more than a few yards, shots rang out. He turned, and as he was running back to the wagons, bullets began coming from all directions. Each family went to their wagon for protection and armed themselves. Considering the distance and rapid fire, Uncle Owen told some of the men he felt they were using the new Henry repeaters. There were some good rifles in the wagon train, but not much to compete with the repeaters.

James and Peter grabbed their Navy 36s and also strapped on their 45s. The gunfire continued off and on for several hours. The Indians were crawling through the grass and getting closer. It was almost impossible to see them until they fired on the wagon train. Several people had been hit and some killed. Many of the animals had also been killed. It seemed not a single one of the Indians had been hit.

Uncle Owen gathered several of the men in the center of the wagons and told them, "We can't hold them off indefinitely. They are crawling in the grasses and getting closer and have us outgunned. The only protection we have is the wagons. Conserve your ammunition, but keep them as far back as possible. I think one of us should ride out and find the soldiers for help."

No one offered a better idea, but also didn't offer to be the one to ride. There were a couple of good strong riding horses on the train. One was especially long-winded, and Uncle Owen said he would attempt it, but explained, under the best of conditions, if he made it, help probably couldn't get back for at least a full day. They would have to try to hold them off for as long as possible. He saddled up, took one container of water, and left his rifle for those at the wagons. He asked Peter and James for their Navy 36s and made sure they were both loaded. He climbed on the horse, and told the family he loved them and would be back with help. He sat low in the saddle and rode out at a full run. As he approached the Indians, he had a revolver in each hand, and all twelve shots could be heard. He made it past them and could be seen riding over the crest. No one pursued him.

Gunfire started up again. James and Peter now had their 45s. Bullets again seemed to be coming from all directions. Most everyone was firing from the protection of their wagons. The boys were moving from one location to the other and using their ammunition sparingly. As they moved around, they found many of the people in the wagons were already wounded or dead. They were both running out of ammunition, and Peter ran to their wagon.

As he looked in, he turned back to James with a face of pain, reached in, and pulled out the last box of 45 ammunition. He ran back to James and gave him half of the ammunition. Then he said, "Don't look in the wagon. Mom and Dad are gone. There is nothing we can do."

The two of them kept moving from wagon to wagon, firing only when they thought they had a good shot. They tried to be as accurate as possible and to conserve their ammunition. But handguns weren't a very good match against the modern repeaters. James saw Peter drop. He fell backward away from one of the wagons. James knelt down next to him. He had blood on the front of his shirt, but at least, there was no look of pain on his face. He felt he had now lost his whole family and would probably not live long enough to see Uncle Owen return. James again loaded and carefully shot. He soon realized the sound of his gun was the only one coming from the wagon train. And then, there was just silence. He was out of ammunition. He holstered his revolver and stood firm in the center of the circle of wagons.

The Indians seemed to come in between the wagons like a flood of water. They all surrounded him. He had tears in his eyes, but it was obvious they were not tears of fear. One of the Indians rode up in front of him and spoke English.

"You have killed and tortured my people. Now you will die."

There was still no fear shown in James's face, only anger and hate. James was standing on the ground, and the Indian was on his horse.

James had to look up, but he spoke as if they were face-to-face. "We hurt no one. Those that hurt your people have been captured by the soldiers and will be punished. Now, you are the ones that will be hunted. And my spirit will watch you be punished."

The Indian seemed to stare into his eyes for minutes without a word and then said, "For so few years, you have the strength of an elder. We will honor you and not take your life. If the soldiers will punish those that hurt my people, we will no longer seek revenge."

He turned to the others and spoke in his language. They began picking up any bodies that were on the ground and put them in wagons and then set them on fire. One of the Indians walked over to Peter and started to drag him to a wagon. James ran and clipped him from behind and knocked him to the ground. Another Indian grabbed James and threw him to the side. As he did, Albert came out of nowhere and lunged at him catching his arm in his mouth. The Indian screamed and tried to throw the dog off. James was up and told Albert no; he stopped immediately. James told them to leave him where he was. The English speaker asked why, and James explained it was his brother and he didn't want him burnt. James then asked them not to hurt the dog and to leave him with his brother. The English speaker spoke to the others, and they finished setting fire to the last of the wagons. One of the Indians brought a horse with a saddle on it over to James. The horse had been saddled that morning and was one of the few that hadn't been shot. He then motioned for James to get on. He was still wearing his Colt but felt they knew it was empty, so it was no threat to them. As the Indians started to leave, the Indian that brought him the horse started leading it by the reins and took him with them. They had only gone about a half mile, and the English speaker said something, and they all stopped. The reins were handed to James, and they started riding off again. James rode with them.

CHAPTER 3

Tragedy Discovered

Uncle Owen and the soldiers didn't arrive until the following morning. From a distance, it was obvious they were arriving too late. They could see the wagons had been burned to the ground. The fires were already out. Uncle Owen was sick to his stomach; he felt he had failed. As they rode into what was left of the circle of wagons, they found one survivor, Peter, laying up against a wheel with a canteen and Albert the dog at his side. He was bloody but alive.

Uncle Owen ran over to him. Peter looked up at him and smiled. Albert was lying against him but wagging his tail at the sight of Uncle Owen.

Peter's face then changed as he told Uncle Owen, "I think everyone is dead. I've called out, but no one's answered. I've only moved enough to get to this canteen. I've been hit in the side, but the bullet seems to have gone through." Peter paused for several seconds. "Uncle Owen, I'm scared. They're gone. They're all gone. Mom, Dad, and James, they are all gone."

Uncle Owen was on his knees with his hand on Peter's shoulder. He stood up and went to his horse, retrieved a canteen, and returned to Peter. He poured some water in his hat and handed the canteen to Peter. He let Albert drink from his hat. Peter gulped at the canteen and then wet his hands to rinse his face.

"We'll get you patched up the best we can and get you to the Fort. But I think we better wait a couple of days until you're strong enough to travel." Uncle Owen gave him as much encouragement as possible, but knew it would take more than that to cure his broken heart.

Most of the wagons were just piles of burnt debris. Many of the bodies were burned so badly that you couldn't distinguish between the men and the women. The soldiers spent the rest of the day digging a large grave and burying the bodies. They covered the common grave with rocks and made a permanent marker. No one actually counted the bodies, and the absence of a body thought to be James's was not noticed. Most of the animals had also been killed. The ones that hadn't were simply let loose to forge on their own. Uncle Owen kept the two surviving mules and two of the cows.

With only the passing of one day, Peter felt he was already gaining strength. But the pain seemed to be worse. Uncle Owen said that was normal for the first few days after such a severe injury. Uncle Owen and Albert stayed by Peter's side and made sure he had plenty of food, water, and encouragement.

CHAPTER 4

Escape to the North

James was riding in the middle of the group of Indians. He had no idea where they were going or what they intended to do with him. But he was not going to allow them to see any fear. After several miles, he pulled his horse to a stop. The Indians quickly maneuvered into a circle around him.

James asked, "Where are we going, and why am I with you?" He looked straight at the English-speaking Indian and with a determined look asked again, "Where are you taking me?"

The Indians also all looked at the English speaker. James felt he was the leader or the chief or in some position of authority. For some reason, James almost felt a bond and then began to be angry with himself for feeling anything for a person that had killed his entire family.

The Indian said, "We are going to the hills. First we have to lead the soldiers in a different direction and then cover our tracks. We are taking you to our village to see who we are and why our hate was so strong. When you have learned this, we will let you go."

They turned their horses and started moving again. Within an hour, they came to a small river. It was wide, but not deep, maybe about two feet in the middle. They entered the water at an angle to the right. The English-speaking Indian spoke, and half of the Indians crossed the river and went up the other bank and turned right. They moved parallel with the river and after a few hundred yards went back in again. They came back staying in the water and then made the circle again. They did this several times. The rest went in the opposite direction and staying in the middle of the river leaving no trace. The English speaker told James they would do this in several locations. They separate and go different directions and cover their trails and meet later in the evening. The group James was with traveled a couple of miles in the river and then moved inland in an area where the ground was hard enough to hide the tracks. Some tracts were left but could barely be seen. He doubted anyone would find them. James had tried to think of ways to deliberately leave a trail but for some reason was now glad he hadn't. They traveled until about an hour after dark and then stopped to rest the animals and eat. The food was mostly just dried strips of meat, some type of stale flatbread, and of course water. Within a short time, the other Indians joined them. The horses were allowed to graze but had both front legs tied together at the fetlock with about six inches of slack. James unsaddled his horse and made sure it had water. They all talked for what James thought was about an hour, then lay down to go to sleep. James lay down but had nothing to keep him warm. The night was getting cold. He thought once he fell asleep, he wouldn't notice the cold. After a few minutes, he sensed someone standing over him. He looked up. It was one of the Indians, just looking at him. Then he dropped a blanket down and walked off. The Indian had been watching him all day. He looked about fourteen but very alert about his surroundings.

Before the Indian had lain back down, James said, "Thank you." Then he realized the Indian probably had no idea what he said, but probably understood by the tone of his voice. His mind started racing again. Why could he be so full of anger, and yet understanding and almost feeling a sympathy for the loss of family and friends the Indians had experienced? They were feeling the same loss he was experiencing. He wondered if he had too much of his mother's kindness. What would his father or Uncle Owen think or do?

Before light, everyone was up. He walked over to the fourteen-year-old Indian and tried to give the blanket back, but he wouldn't take it. They ate lightly again. When James saddled his horse, he tied the blanket to the back of the saddle and looked at the fourteen-year-old and nodded. They all mounted and rode off going north. Two Indians remained behind, one on each rear flank. They would stay behind and off to the side, never getting above any crest behind them. James knew it prevented their silhouette from being seen with the sky as a backdrop. It appeared this was all done to make sure they were not followed.

It was another day of riding until dark. When they made camp, the two riding behind stayed behind and watched. Making camp was the same as the night before. The animals were secured and given water and allowed to graze. The Indians then ate their dried meat and bread, talked, and even laughed. Within a short time, they went to sleep. James had listened to as much of the conversation as he could to see if he could learn any of the language. He lay there on the ground for a few minutes, then turned and looked over to the fourteen-year-old Indian. They made eye contact, James nodded, and so did the Indian. James had been feeling hollow due to the loss of his family, especially since he was riding with those that murdered them. But somehow, the fourteen-year-old's nod filled a small portion of that loss. He then closed his eyes and fell asleep.

CHAPTER 5

Strength Returns

Three days had passed, and there didn't appear to be any infection in Peter's wound. With the bullet going through, there was no digging to be done saving him the additional pain and damage to the wound. Uncle Owen had cleaned it the best he could, and before dressing it, they had put a few stitches in to help close the hole. Fortunately, it appeared that no organs had been hit. He cleaned the wound every morning and redressed it with a clean cloth he had washed in boiled water.

Uncle Owen cooked meat from the cow they had lost. With the meat, plenty of water, and some dry goods left by the soldiers, they were eating well. And Peter's youth was helping him heal quickly.

The soldiers left on the second morning after burying the victims. It was now the fourth morning, and Uncle Owen asked Peter if he thought he was strong enough to start toward Fort Kearny.

Peter answered, "I'm feeling strong, and I need to get out of here. Everything I look at is a reminder that Mom, Dad, and James are gone. All I have to remember James by is the Colt you gave us. I spent some time poking through the ashes, but couldn't find it."

Uncle Owen said, "It was probably burned so badly that you wouldn't have recognized it. The nickel would have melted or blackened, and the grips would have burned off. We have two of the mules, two cows, and of course, Albert. We need to feel fortunate for that. We'll leave in the morning and take our time traveling."

For the last three days, Peter had been constantly getting up and moving about. He felt keeping his muscles moving and his blood flowing helped him keep his strength up and heal the wound quicker. It seemed to be working.

The following morning, they packed up a few items that survived the fires and put them on one of the mules. Peter was to ride the long-winded horse, and Uncle Owen would ride the other mule with the two cows in tow. Taking their time, it took them four days to get to Dobytown, the small community next to the old fort. The fort and the town were almost completely abandoned, but a few families had remained behind. They were mostly just farmers. One of the soldiers had returned from the wagon train massacre and told them of the attack and that there was only one survivor, an eleven-year-old named Peter, and he would be coming with his uncle.

Dobytown had once been a bustling community, but was nothing now. The railroad had changed everything in the area. A town was built on the opposite side of the river and named Kearney after the fort. The *e* was added to the name by a mistake in a newspaper article and just stuck.

When Uncle Owen and James arrived, they were politely greeted and told by the remaining farmers to settle into one of the abandoned adobe buildings. A solid building was found, and it had a good watertight roof. It afforded them shade during the day and warmth at night. They salvaged a couple of chairs and a table from some of the other vacant buildings, and the adobe building was now a comfortable place to stay. Sleeping on the floor was no problem. They had been sleeping on the ground since leaving Independence. A few of the locals gave them a couple of extra blankets. In exchange, Uncle Owen shared fresh milk from the cows. The cows didn't produce much, but every little bit was appreciated. Before they left, Uncle Owen had salvaged a few cooking utensils, a skillet, a pot with a lid, a couple of plates, and spoons and forks, from the burnt wagons. There was not much else salvageable.

They stayed in Dobytown for a couple of months. Peter was now fully recovered and had been going out hunting for food and just exploring the area. The exercise seemed to help him heal not only physically, but also mentally. And his hatred for the Indians seemed to be diminishing.

One evening, in a conversation about the wagon train and what was to become of them, Uncle Owen told Peter, "The pain of your wound will go away. The pain from the loss of your family will remain, but it will get easier with time. I have confidence you will do well in life and leave your mark."

Uncle Owen told Peter he had a wife. Peter was surprised and said he had never been told.

Uncle Owen said, "I don't talk about it. My wife died a month before you and James were born. She died in childbirth, and I also lost the baby, a son. Even though I never knew him, I still feel the loss of them both. You and James have been my sons. You have given me so much, and I have been so proud of you."

CHAPTER 6

A New Beginning—A New Life

Uncle Owen felt it was time for them to move on and maybe get a job to provide a better life for Peter. With no more than what they had, it didn't take much time to pack up. They tried to give the blankets back to those that had helped them but were told to keep them. Actually, Uncle Owen was glad because they did need them. The cows were left with the farmers. They left for the new town of Kearney. It wasn't much, but was certainly much more than Dobytown. The town was on the north side of the Platt River and south of the new railroad. And it looked as though it would grow. There was also a small school, and Uncle Owen felt this was important for Peter. They spent the first night sleeping just outside of the town. The following morning, Uncle Owen went to town to find work. The first place he went to was the local blacksmith's shop. Uncle Owen had done blacksmith work and was very good. He demonstrated his skill with the forge, shoeing a horse, and repairing some parts on a local farmer's wagon and was hired. The blacksmith was a short, very strong man, with kindness in his eyes and manner of speaking. Uncle Owen talked with him while working and explained what they had been through the last few months.

The blacksmith smiled and said, "Call me Samuel. There is a small room at the rear of the shop. It isn't much, but you and Peter can stay there. Use the well to the side of the shop, and there is an outhouse behind the corrals. It should help you get by until you can save up some money."

Uncle Owen was very appreciative. That evening, Samuel introduced him to the school teacher and enrolled Peter. There were eleven kids of all ages. She taught all grades and said Peter would be no problem. And best of all, there was no cost. She was paid by the city.

Everything was going better than expected, and best of all, it stayed that way. As time went on, they were able to fix up the room and get better clothes. They sold the mules and bought another horse. Peter was doing very well in school and made friends quickly. Samuel told Peter he didn't have enough work to hire him, but knew someone that may. He took Peter down the street and introduced him to Mr. and Mrs. Johnson. They owned the general store. Samuel gave Peter a recommendation, and they agreed to use him on Saturdays.

Mr. Johnson was a tall handsome man, and his wife was extremely nice. Peter soon learned they seemed to know everyone in town and were obviously well-liked. Mr. Johnson was also constantly funny, and they both treated Peter like a son. On Saturdays, while working, the Johnsons would always take a little time to teach him about business and the importance of saving money. They even helped him get a savings account at the bank. Their daughter, Sarah, was Peter's age and also worked in the store. Peter also knew her from school. He thought she was pretty and liked the way she wore her hair in a long dark braid hanging down her back. She was also always smiling and pleasant to everyone.

Peter got close to the county sheriff that came through town once or twice a week. Most people just referred to him as Sheriff Joe.

When he grew up, Peter felt he wanted to be a sheriff. The sheriff would visit him and Uncle Owen in the back of the blacksmith shop and talk to Peter about the law, honor, and how to investigate crimes. They talked about reading people by what they say, how they say it, and their physical movements.

By the time Peter was sixteen, he not only was still working at the general store, but also began working with the sheriff on some of his local cases. Because of his involvement, he also made friends with the territorial judge. Peter was getting well known, building an honorable reputation, and, at his young age, already becoming admired as a lawman. His special Colt had become his trademark. The full-framed, cartridge firing 45s were becoming more popular, but none were like his.

Peter was physically strong and mentally clear-minded. He only seemed to have one problem. On Saturdays, while working at the general store, he worked with the owner's daughter, Sarah. They had become great friends, and she was a constant encouragement for his desire to improve himself. However, at sixteen, she had changed from being pretty to now being the most beautiful young woman he had ever seen. It seemed no matter what he was doing, thoughts of her would come to mind. He just wasn't sure about telling her how he felt, for fear of causing a problem with their relationship.

He discussed it with Uncle Owen, but all he said was "Son, it will work out on its own. Maybe you should ask her how she feels. As close as you two are, I don't believe there is anything that could damage your friendship. You seem to have a bond that most people never experience in a lifetime."

Peter responded, "I can face a man with a gun, but don't have the courage to tell her my feelings. I just can't risk the possibility of losing her friendship. That would be worse than the pain I felt being shot. I've lost everyone but you, and I can't risk losing her."

It was only a couple of days later, and Peter was in the general store picking up a few things. There were no customers, just he and Mrs. Johnson.

All of a sudden, Mrs. Johnson asked, "When are you going to tell Sarah how you feel?" then, looking him straight in the face, smiled and giggled.

He asked, "Is it that obvious? I love her, I've never said that, not even out loud to myself, but I love her. Every time I see her, she gets more beautiful, and my lungs feel like they are going to explode. I think I have loved her all the time and not known it until this last year."

Still looking at him and smiling, she answered, "Well, I can tell you it's obvious to everyone in town. Let her know how you feel. Let her hear it from you. She needs that."

Peter said, "I want to tell her, but just can't seem to get it out."

Mrs. Johnson invited Peter and Uncle Owen over for supper. It had been a little more than a week since he and Mrs. Johnson had talked about Sarah. Her suppers were the best in town, and James and Uncle Owen were usually asked over several times a month.

About halfway through the meal, Mr. Johnson said, "Peter, even though you are not our son, we want you to know how proud of you we are. When Samuel first brought you over and recommended you for a job, Mrs. Johnson and I both felt you would become a fine young man. And you have done just that."

Peter answered, "That's quite a compliment coming from you, and I hope you know how much I appreciate and respect both of you. My last five years here in Kearney have gone well. What you have taught me and the example you have set are a large part of why things have gone so well for me. I think I have everything I could ask for, except one thing. I just need Sarah."

He surprised everyone with the comment about Sarah, especially Sarah. But it was obvious from the look on her face, she was more than pleased, which somewhat put Peter at ease after the comment he had just blurted out.

Mrs. Johnson snickered and said, "Well, isn't that interesting."

Then everyone just continued to eat but kept smiling and grinning. Peter had embarrassed himself but felt he had at least said it, and now Sarah knew how he felt.

CHAPTER 7

Life Gets Even Better

For the next two years, Peter worked more closely with the sheriff. He also completed local legal obligations for the territorial judge. He was receiving wages for both jobs and also still working periodically at the general store for the Johnsons. Peter and Sarah had been growing even closer and were now planning their wedding. Peter had plans for purchasing one of the homes on the outskirts of town. It was a small home but extremely well-built with a small additional living space at the rear. It was on a couple of acres and had a large stable for protecting the animals and storing feed during the winter. Peter had plans for Uncle Owen to live with them, and the extra space would be perfect. Sarah was fine with that. She was also close to Uncle Owen. She even called him Uncle Owen, and he seemed to like that.

One evening while cleaning up the kitchen, Sarah was talking to her mother about how much she cared for Peter. Her mother smiled and asked Sarah if she noticed how long the barrel was on his revolver. Sarah gave her a puzzled look and asked, "What has that to do with anything?"

Her mother said, "Some women say you can tell how big a man is by the length of his barrel."

Sarah just gasped and said "Mother, I can't believe you said that."

Her mother just laughed and said, "It's not true. If it was, women would only marry men who carried shotguns."

Sarah was shocked at what her mother was telling her but burst out laughing.

Peter had worked with Sheriff Joe on not only minor legal problems around town, but also quelling fights at the local saloon. Some of these confrontations were getting more and more troublesome. Most of these were the result of cowboys having too much to drink. One time, in a past conversation with the sheriff, Peter was told about a local cattle rancher, Wes Franklin. Sheriff Joe said Franklin had moved in the area soon after Fort Kearny had been retired by the Army.

He told Peter, "This is a good place to raise cattle. There is plenty of water from the Platt River, good grassland, and it is close to the railroad for shipping the cattle to market. The problem is Mr. Franklin. He hires the worst of the cowboys."

He also told Peter, "It was Franklin's cowboys that attacked the Indian village and caused the skirmish that resulted in the attack on your wagon train."

Sheriff Joe stressed those cowboys were an example of the men Franklin hired. With a very serious look on his face, he then told Peter, "When any of Franklin's cowboys are in town, always be aware of your surroundings and where they are. I don't trust them, and I don't want you to."

CHAPTER 8

Kearney Gets Tough

Uncle Owen had been sent out to one of the ranches to shoe some of the horses and do some repair work on a plow and other farm equipment. The blacksmith's shop had a wagon with a forge attached to it and was used for just this purpose. The job took Owen three days to complete. On his way back to the blacksmith's shop, Uncle Owen stopped at the saloon. He was tired, hot, dirty, and felt like a beer before he cleaned up and got some rest. He gave a hello to the owner, Tom, walked over and sat in the corner, and they talked about how tired he was. He hadn't been in the saloon long before three new cowboys came in. They were loud, boisterous, and rude to Tom.

Owen spoke up and said, "Since you men are new to town, I'll give you some helpful advice. People here are respectful of each other. It will serve you well to be respectful back."

One of the three cowboys, obviously the youngest, turned and loudly said, "We don't need any advice from an old man." He took a few steps toward the table and pushed it out of the way with his boot. He had a full view of Owen sitting in the chair with the beer in his hand. He then said, "Why would someone shoot their mouth off and not carry a gun?"

Tom came out from behind the bar. As soon as he started to speak, the young cowboy told him to get back and mind his own business.

Owen looked over at Tom with a smile and said, "It's okay, Tom. All is fine."

The young cowboy again asked, "Why don't you have a gun, old man?"

Owen responded, "I'm a blacksmith, and there is no need to have one."

The cowboy turned to one of the others and told him to take his gun belt off. He then took it and tossed it on the table Owen had been using. He took a step back and told Owen to put it on. Tom spoke up again, and the cowboy snapped back, saying, "Shut up and don't you move."

Owen looked at Tom, nodded his head, and again said, "Everything will be okay."

Tom, looking at Owen, asked if he should go get Joe, and the cowboy snapped back that he had told him not to move. The cowboy then told Owen to put the gun belt on. Owen put his beer on the table, put the belt on, and made a joke about it being a little too tight.

The cowboy said, "Let's see how good you are with it."

Owen very clumsily pulled the gun out of the holster like he had not handled one very much before. He fumbled with it and cocked it with both hands, and the gun went off, blowing a hole in the floor just an inch in front of the young cowboy's boot. Owen appeared startled and quickly put the gun back in the holster.

The young cowboy, visibly upset, said, "You fool, you almost blew my foot off. You're lucky I haven't already killed you."

Owen asked, "What am I supposed to do with the gun?"

The cowboy replied, "You're going to draw on me."

Tom was almost in a panic and started for the door. The cowboy drew and fired a shot in front of him and said he had told him not to move.

Owen again said, "Tom, it will be okay. Don't worry."

The cowboy told Owen he had better be worried. Owen asked if he could practice just a little more. The cowboy started to laugh, and Owen pulled the gun faster than he could respond. As the gun came out, his left hand went across the hammer with just a blur. Three shots rang out, the shots landing just in front of each cowboy's boots. Owen then twirled the revolver once and pointed it at the young cowboy's head. Owen smiled and said, "I think I've had enough practice. I have two shots left, one for you and one for the man still with a gun belt." He then holstered the gun and waited a minute before taking off the belt and handing it back to the unarmed cowboy. Then looking at the three cowboys, he said, "I think maybe you should go now."

Without a word, all three cowboys turned and left.

Tom said, "I thought I was going to have a heart attack. I've not seen them before. I bet they are new men hired out at the Franklin ranch."

Owen told Tom he was sorry about the holes in the floor and would repair them. Tom just said, "Leave them. They'll make for a good story over a drink."

One afternoon, another fight had broken out in the saloon. Peter was in town and went with the sheriff. Guns had been drawn and a couple of shots fired, but no one was hit. When the sheriff and Peter walked in, it was obvious the tension was at the point someone was about to be killed. The sheriff and Peter both pulled their guns and demanded the others holster theirs. Three of the cowboys didn't. The sheriff gave one last command. Two of the cowboys holstered, but the third quickly spun toward the sheriff.

As he did, a shot rang out, and he fell backward to the floor. The sheriff had hit him directly in the center of the chest. He didn't die immediately, but gasped for air and then went limp. The other two cowboys were told to unbelt their guns and let them drop to the floor. They did as they were told. The sheriff told the bartender to get the doctor. Peter instinctively walked around behind the two cowboys, being careful not to get between them and the sheriff. With his foot, he kicked both gun belts to the side and picked them up.

Peter and Sheriff Joe walked the two cowboys across the street to the small sheriff's office almost directly across from the saloon. The office was a single room with a desk and three chairs. At the rear of the office were a back door, a six-by-eight cell with a steel bar door on the front and a one-foot-square barred window at the rear. The only furnishings were a commode pot and a single bunk.

Sheriff Joe put the two men in the cell, and Peter hung their gun belts on the wall, and then they both returned to the saloon. The doctor officially pronounced the cowboy dead and asked if anyone knew his name. There were two other cowboys, still in the saloon. They gave the doctor the information he needed and told him they were all from the Franklin Ranch. The doctor had the body removed and told the sheriff he would have him buried. Tom was now at the saloon. He looked at Sheriff Joe and told him the young man he had just shot was the same one who had tried to pick a fight with Owen.

Sheriff Joe turned to the two cowboys and said, "Go back to the ranch and tell Franklin the men in jail will remain there until the judge comes through town next week. Also, tell Mr. Franklin I don't want to see any of his men in town until after the judge arrives."

The cowboys were polite, caused no trouble, and left.

The following morning, Peter was in town going to the general store. Just before entering the front door, he saw Sheriff Joe on the walk across the street, gave a verbal greeting, and then stepped inside. Mr. Johnson was behind the counter and smiled as Peter walked in. Then Mr. Johnson got a strange look on his face as he looked over Peter's shoulder. Peter turned to look out the front windows. Sheriff Joe was stepping into the street with his gun in his hand, but not raised. Peter looked to his left and saw a group of about ten men on horseback coming down the street. Peter didn't have his Colt. He stepped behind the counter and picked up a 45 that was for sale. He quickly loaded it, stuck it in his belt, grabbed a ten-gauge shotgun off the shelf, loaded it, and walked out the door.

As he stepped out the door, he turned and said to Mr. Johnson, "Stay behind the counter and away from the glass."

Sheriff Joe was already in the middle of the street. As the men rode up in front of him, Peter recognized Franklin as the man on the front horse. The men seemed to pay no mind to Peter still on the boardwalk to their right side.

Franklin looked directly down to Sheriff Joe and said, "No one tells me or my men we can't come to town. We are here for the men you are holding, to have a drink at the saloon, and we're not leaving until we are ready. If need be, we'll ride past your dead body."

Peter had not realized what a threat Franklin was until now. Peter stepped off the walkway and walked over and stood by Sheriff Joe.

Without taking his eyes off the riders, Sheriff Joe said, "I have this, Peter. This is my job."

Peter was staring into Franklin's eyes and said, "This is our job."

Franklin, looking down from his horse, said, "Young man, do you realize you may die here?"

Peter quickly answered, "I made that decision when I walked into the street. But no matter how this turns out, you will be the first to die. Have you noticed this shotgun is aimed directly at your chest and both hammers are back? The first man that moves, I am pulling both triggers and will splatter you all over everyone behind you. Now the question is, are you willing to die here?"

Franklin's face filled with anger. While still looking down at Peter, Franklin said, "Men, we are going back to the ranch."

Peter cut in and said, "They leave now. You stay here until they are at the edge of town. Then you can go."

Mr. Franklin told his men, "Start back to the ranch. I'll catch up with you outside of town." He then looked at Sheriff Joe and Peter. "You have not heard the end of this. No one tells me what I can and can't do."

Peter, looking him in the eyes, said, "Then you better get your own town. This one belongs to the people of Kearney."

Sheriff Joe and Peter both waited a minute and then told Mr. Franklin he could leave. He turned his horse and slowly rode away. Sheriff Joe turned and looked at Peter, "Oh shit, son, you have more iron in your spine than the blacksmith's shop. I may be alive because of you."

Mr. Johnson stepped out of the store door and off the boardwalk. As he came up to Peter, he said, "I hope I never have to see anything like that again. Did you know that shotgun is in for repair and sometimes doesn't work?"

Peter said, "No, and I'm glad I didn't until now."

The sheriff laughed and said, "Son, you know I don't like to curse, but I think I have to say 'oh shit' again."

Peter never said a word to Sarah about the incident. But within a few days, it became obvious Mr. Johnson had. With no warning, Sarah walked up to Peter, got face-to-face, and said, "I heard about you. We're getting married, and I'm not waiting. It's going to be now. We have the money to get the mortgage for the house. You love me uncontrollably, and we're getting married. I spoke to the preacher about an hour ago, and the arrangements are being made. By the way, Uncle Owen is excited for you."

Peter laughed; all he could think was, *She has more iron in her spine than Sheriff Joe said I have.* Peter laughed and just said, "Wow, what a woman I'm about to marry. You're as strong as you are beautiful, and I like that."

She knew by the grin on his face he was glad and was to be her husband shortly.

CHAPTER 9

A Real Family—A Real Home

Sarah and Peter were married within the next two days. The people selling the house were leaving shortly, and the timing was perfect. The people moving were also leaving some of the furniture. For the last year, Sarah had been collecting many of the household goods they would be needing. For being young, they were starting out with a fairly well-furnished house.

One evening while closing the general store, Sarah and Peter were alone. He turned to her in the dark, and she could see tears in his eyes.

She was concerned and asked, "What's the matter? Is everything all right?"

Peter didn't say anything for several seconds and then answered, "I am so in love with you. My life couldn't be any better."

The district judge came to town for the trial of the two cowboys being held in the jail. The killing of the cowboy by Sheriff Joe was found to be a justified homicide. The two cowboys were found guilty of disorderly conduct and assault with a deadly weapon. Since they holstered their weapons when asked by the sheriff, the judge sentenced them to one week in jail but considered time waiting for trial as the week served. Sheriff Joe was satisfied.

They were both released, and it was also a lot of trouble keeping them in the small cell. Franklin didn't show up for the trial, but there were three unfamiliar faces in the courtroom. Sheriff Joe believed they were Franklin's men. To confirm this, he walked over to them and told them to tell Franklin he and his men were now welcome back in town. They just nodded and walked out of the courtroom, got on horses out front, and left town. That confirmed and satisfied Sheriff Joe's curiosity.

The two freed cowboys were walked back over to the office, given their guns, and allowed to leave town. After the two cowboys left, Sheriff Joe looked at Peter and said, "I didn't like the looks of those three unfamiliar men in the courtroom. They weren't cowboys. They dressed differently, their guns and holsters were well maintained, and their hands did not show evidence of hard work. If you see them in town, don't turn your back on them. They gave me a bad feeling."

CHAPTER 10

A Painful Loss Again

For the next week, everything seemed to go well. But late one evening, Albert started to bark. Within a moment, someone was banging on the front door and hollering Peter's name. He recognized the voice as the doctor's. He quickly got up, hollered, "Just a minute," lit a lamp, and went to the door.

When he opened it, the doctor pushed his way into the house. He looked Peter in the face and said, "Sheriff Joe has been shot. He was walking across the street and was shot from behind. There was nothing I could do for him. Before he died, all he said was 'Tell Peter to be careful, an iron spine can't stop a bullet.' I didn't want you to hear it from anyone else."

Sarah was awake; he told her he had to go with the doctor and would be back in an hour or two. He explained Sheriff Joe had been shot, but not to wake Uncle Owen. He would tell him in the morning.

Peter left with the doctor. They went straight to the doctor's office where Sheriff Joe was lying faceup on a table in the middle of his exam room. His eyes were closed but showed pain on his face.

Peter looked at the doctor and said, "I need all the information I can get. I want the bullet, information on where it entered, how deep it went in the body. Anything you can think of. But first, show me exactly where the sheriff was and how you found him lying."

The doctor took him out into the street. There were still some people standing around talking about the sheriff and asking questions. The doctor showed him the spot.

Peter asked, "Show me how he was laying, what way his head was facing, and anything that comes to mind."

The doctor drew a stick figure in the dirt showing how he found the sheriff. "He was face down, and all he could tell me was what he said to tell you. He then died. I asked if anyone had moved him and was told no."

Peter told him he could go back to the office and then turned to look at the men standing around. In the group of men were two of the men Sheriff Joe had warned him about. Peter asked if anyone had seen the shooting or been outside when the sheriff was shot. No one had any information. They all said they came out when they heard a shot. One said he came out later when he heard the commotion and voices.

Peter stepped up to get face-to-face with the two men he was suspicious of. He asked to see their revolvers. They didn't question his request; they simply handed him their revolvers. He smelled the barrels, and neither had been fired recently. He examined the weapons a little more closely. They both had custom grips and were spotless. One grip had six notches, but they were on the inside grip so as not to be seen when holstered. He didn't say a word, just handed the revolvers back. The one with the notched revolver asked if he could see Peter's. Peter just looked at him. Peter asked, "Where's your third friend? I never see you three separated."

The one he had just handed the gun to told him he was at the saloon enjoying a drink. Peter walked over to the saloon, entered through the front door, and looked around. There were only three people in the room. Two of them Peter knew well and would not have been involved. The third had been at the trial and was one of the three Sheriff Joe had warned him to look out for. He was the one Peter was looking for. Peter walked over to him and asked to see his revolver. The man gently pulled it out and handed it butt first to Peter. It obviously hadn't been fired either.

When he handed it back, the man asked, "Want to trade?"

Peter just turned and walked away remembering Sheriff Joe telling him to watch his back. As he walked out, he could see the man's reflection in the window at the front of the saloon.

He did not appear to be of any threat. Peter had a question for the bartender, but didn't want to ask in front of the man.

He walked back down the street to the doctor's office. He felt he was boiling over with anger but, worst of all, was frustrated at the thought of not finding who pulled the trigger. He opened the front door and stepped in. As he did, he looked at the doctor's face and could see the loss in his eyes. Sheriff Joe was also a very good friend of his. He told the doctor to go home and get some sleep. He could wait until the morning to retrieve the bullet and get him the information he needed. Peter added, "I need to get some sleep too. I'll give you time in the morning to see what information you can get. Hopefully, something that can help us. I don't mean to sound so cold and matter of fact, but I have to keep a clear head. I'm going to get this son of a bitch, and he will pay dearly."

Peter then left the office. While walking home, he was feeling the same loss and anger as when he was eleven and was the only survivor of the wagon train. Only this time, he was determined to get revenge.

When he got back to the house, Sarah and Uncle Owen were both up. Uncle Owen had heard the noise when the doctor came and had gotten up just as Peter left. It was easy for the two of them to see how upset Peter was. He looked at them, paused for a moment, and said, "He was shot from behind while walking across the street. They shot him in the back. He warned me something like this could happen. Somehow, someway, they will get their due justice."

Sarah felt sick to her stomach. She loved Sheriff Joe and was also thinking the same thing could happen to Peter. She looked at Peter, waited for a second, and said, "Should we leave here? They can do the same to you. You wouldn't have a chance. Peter, I can't lose you. I would die from the inside out."

Peter took a step forward and held her for a moment and then looked at the pain in her face. He told her, "Our lives are not guaranteed. We need to live them with purpose. You are my purpose, but this town and the safety of those in it is also my purpose. I can't leave, Sarah."

She didn't like his answer, but understood.

There were few men like him, and she loved him for it.

The following morning, Peter went to town with Uncle Owen at his side. He trusted Uncle Owen's advice and shrewd thinking. He went to the sheriff's office and went through his desk. He told Uncle Owen, "I'm looking for something that might give me an indication, or an idea, as to anything Sheriff Joe was investigating or concerned about." There was nothing.

While walking over to the doctor's office, Peter told Uncle Owen, "Starting today, I'm keeping a diary as a record of everything I do and any suspicions I might have. It not only can help me in court cases but also might help if anything was to happen to me."

The doctor had already been in for several hours. Sheriff Joe was cleaned up, and the doctor said they were making a box for him. Peter started asking questions. "Did you find the bullet?"

The doctor showed him what he had retrieved. The bullet was distorted, but the caliber was easily determined as a 45. Uncle Owen picked up the bullet and examined it a little more closely. He told Peter, "Because of the heavier weight, I think it's the newer government 45-70. Look at the tip. It has been mushroomed out more than normal. I think the tip had an *X* cut in it to make the bullet mushroom. See how each side is mushroomed out almost the same amount with even splits." He pulled out one of his bullets and had the doctor give him a dull knife. He notched the tip of the bullet with an *X* and then took the tip of the knife and twisted it into the center to create a small hole. Then showing it to Peter, he explained why it would spread out more on impact.

Peter looked at the bullet and put it in his pocket. He became angry with himself. He told Uncle Owen and the doctor, "I can't believe I didn't think to check rifles last night. There were three men Sheriff Joe warned me about. I checked their revolvers, and they hadn't been fired, but I didn't check the rifles. I'm sure any rifle used would have been cleaned by now after seeing me check the revolvers." He then asked the doctor more questions. Such as, could he determine what angle the bullet struck him.

The doctor said, "The bullet hit him in the right arm, just below the elbow, then went through his side damaging his kidneys and liver. It stayed in a straight line traveling even with the line of his belt."

Peter looked at Uncle Owen. "It sounds like the shot was taken from a crouched position. I want to see if we can find where the shot came from. There might be something left behind."

Uncle Owen agreed; they both thanked the doctor and left the office.

They walked to the area where the doctor had found the sheriff. Peter told Uncle Owen about the position the sheriff was in when the doctor found him. They followed a line from the right side of the sheriff down the street. There were just too many places and too many objects a man could crouch down behind, take an easy shot, and not be seen. They looked for a shell casing or anything else that could be of help, but nothing was found. Peter told Uncle Owen he would meet him at the sheriff's office, then walked to the general store.

As soon as he entered, Mr. Johnson told him how sorry he was to hear about the sheriff. Peter nodded; he knew the Johnsons were also good friends with Sheriff Joe. He got some paper to start his diary and left. Peter then stopped at the telegraph office and had a message sent to the district judge reporting Sheriff Joe's murder. Peter finally got to the sheriff's office. He started writing everything down he could remember, including details of the three men from the trial that Sheriff Joe had warned him about and that all three were in town when the sheriff was shot.

Peter and Uncle Owen went back to the house and had a light meal. Sarah was still upset, but as Peter knew, she was an incredibly strong woman. That was only one of the reasons Peter loved her so much. He knew she not only was a remarkable wife but also would be a remarkable mother.

Later in the day, he went to the saloon, hoping to see if the bartender from last evening would be there. He wasn't, but Peter was told he would be in a little later. Peter walked up and down the street asking if anyone had seen or heard anything that might be of help. No one had any information. Later in the afternoon, he went back to the saloon. The bartender from the night before was there. Peter asked him, "When I came in last night, I checked a man's revolver. Do you remember him?"

The bartender said, "Yes, he came in earlier with two other Franklin men. They spent some time in here, and then the one you spoke to left for maybe an hour. We heard the shot from outside, and everyone went out to look. The man you talked to came back in by himself just after everyone else went outside. The other two men are regulars, and they came in just before you did."

Peter thanked him, went to the sheriff's office, and wrote in the diary. He was so upset that he hadn't checked the rifles. He asked himself why he hadn't thought of one of the most logical things to do. It would be dark before he could get out to the Franklin ranch. He decided he would do that tomorrow, after the funeral.

CHAPTER 11

Justice Comes Quickly

The next morning, the funeral was held for Sheriff Joe. The whole town showed up to show their respect. Mr. Wes Franklin was there with his cowhands and the three that Joe had warned him about. The three watched Peter more than the preacher. Uncle Owen had walked to the other side of the grave. Peter knew what he was up to. If there was any problem with the Franklin men, Uncle Owen had now placed them in a cross fire.

After the funeral, many of the townspeople expressed their condolences to Peter. They knew how close the two were. After a few minutes, they began to file out of the graveyard and back toward town. The only exception was Franklin and his men. With Uncle Owen off to their side, Peter walked to the man he had seen in the saloon last night. He asked which horse was his. The man got a puzzled look and then nodded toward a bay mare. Peter walked over to the horse, pulled a rifle from the scabbard, and ejected a shell. It was a 45-70, but the most striking was the *X* cut in the tip of the bullet. Peter put the bullet in his shirt pocket, held the rifle in his left hand, looked at the man, and said, "I am taking the rifle as evidence, and you are under arrest for the murder of Sheriff Joe."

Franklin snapped back, "No one is being arrested, and we're leaving. Put the man's rifle back."

Peter moved his head slightly so he could see both men at the same time and then said, "I am arresting him. If you get involved, I will arrest you too. Is that understood?"

Just then, the eyes and the muscles in the man's neck tightened. Peter knew the man he was arresting was going for his gun. Peter had a habit of turning his body as he drew his gun. The other man was able to shoot first, but the bullet missed Peter's left side by less than an inch. Peter's shot hit the man just below the throat. He fell back into the grave and on Sheriff Joe's casket. Blood spurted from his mouth as he tried to gasp for air. His eyes were wide open and showed panic. Then he went limp. As fast as Peter shot, he turned toward Mr. Franklin, still holding his gun in his hand. "Is there a problem?"

Franklin turned to his men and told them to saddle up. The two other gunmen turned their horses to face Peter. They just stared, then turned back, and rode off with the others. The man Peter had shot laid dead in the grave, on top of the casket. His blood pooled just above Sheriff Joe's feet. Peter felt justified but still felt the loss of Joe who had meant so much to him and had taught him so much. He then turned to Uncle Owen and thanked him. He said, "Without you noticing the notches in the bullet, I would never have caught Joe's murder. Uncle Owen, you have saved me, taught me, protected me, and always been there for me and Sarah. I hope you know how much I appreciate you as my family."

Uncle Owen said nothing; he just put his hand on Peter's shoulder, then turned, and walked away.

During the following two years, the town seemed peaceful even when Franklin and his crew came to town. They made no trouble. The two gunmen always seemed to watch Peter, but everything stayed calm. The general store did well, and the Johnsons were excited to be the grandparents of a handsome young boy. Peter and Sarah named him James.

CHAPTER 12

Family by Choice

They had been riding north for several days, and James sensed a companionship with the fourteen-year-old. As they rode, the fourteen-year-old was always at his left side. He was beginning to feel some strange bond of trust between them. They hadn't spoken and didn't make much eye contact, but James trusted him.

One evening, the fourteen-year-old was looking at his revolver. James called the English speaker over. James pulled the revolver out, looked at the fourteen-year-old, and said, "This was given to me by my uncle. My brother had one just like it. This is all I have. Your people killed my brother and my family."

The English speaker told the young Indian what he said, and then the young man spoke to the English speaker, and then he spoke to James. "It wasn't your family, but your people killed my family. All I have left is my sister. Why?"

James didn't know what to say. He thought for a moment then told the English speaker, "The Army told us about the raid on your village. It was wrong, and we all felt sad. The Army told us there were six men. They found them, three were killed, and the other three will be punished."

The English-speaking Indian told the young Indian. He stayed there for a moment and then got up and walked away. When they rode off the following morning, the fourteen-year-old was again riding next to him. There was a younger girl always riding behind them.

James believed this to be his younger sister. She had long dark hair and a pretty face and seemed to be a hard worker. But he had not seen her smile, not once.

After they stopped for the evening and eaten, James spoke to the English speaker. "If I am to be with you, I need to speak your language. Help me learn. My name is James."

The English speaker said, "My name is Akicita. You would say warrior."

James then asked, "What is the name of the young Indian?"

Akicita told him, "Peyjunta. It means medicine. He seems to help those in need."

They also discussed a few useful phrases to get him started. Akicita then told James, "You will now be known as Tonka James. That is Big James. You have big spirit."

James asked what Peyjunta's sister's name was. Akicita told him, "Anpetu, it is like sun. She shines on others and gives warmth."

They continued riding north for another week. James listened closely and began picking up words and short phrases. He tried talking to Peyjunta; he not only seemed to respect his curiosity of the language but also helped. In fact, Peyjunta was also learning some English words.

Their bond continued to grow. James had no fear of him and felt he could be trusted.

Even though the days seemed calm and he accepted the friendship of Peyjunta, there were several nights James had woken up with anger boiling over inside of him. He could see his brother lying on the ground and the wagons being set on fire with the others inside. He had thoughts flash through his mind of how he could kill some of these people before they killed him. Then he would think of the young girl and how she must feel the same loss for her family. She has her brother, but the others are gone. He understood why he never saw her smile. His anger would change to sadness, and he would fall back to sleep. The next thing he would know he was waking up to the sound of others moving around. The sun would soon be up, and it was time to get ready to move on.

They arrived at a large valley with a small river running through it. There were several groups of tepees, each group having a fire in the middle. Several tepees also had fires inside because he could see indications of smoke coming from the tops. James guessed there were about one hundred Indians. They all came out to greet them and were studying James from a distance; others just came up to him and stared.

He looked at them and said, "Lay he hun nee key wash tay." It was "This morning is good."

They were surprised to hear him use their language. Akicita heard him speak and had a proud look on his face. He listened to Akicita talk to them and believed he was telling them about the wagon train raid. He heard Akicita say Tonka James and then look directly at him.

There was already a group of tepees set up for them. James believed it was done by some of the survivors of the raided village. James was shown where he would be sleeping. He would be staying in the same tepee with Peyjunta and Anpetu Wi. Anpetu Wi was already starting the fire and laying out blankets.

The next morning, Peyjunta brought their two horses to the front of the tepee. He motioned for James to get on one, and they both rode off together. They spent a couple of hours making a circle around the valley. Peyjunta showed him some of the game, where they fished, and some areas with what looked like berry bushes. This valley was much better than any of the places the wagon train had made camp. Before they returned, Peyjunta pulled out his rifle and shot a deer. They hung the animal in a tree, drained it, cleaned it, and kept the hide. He took two long branches and made a travois. Peyjunta stretched the hide across the two branches and made a cradle to hold the meat. They then rode back to the village. By the time they got back to the village, it was already late afternoon. Anpetu Wi must have known they were bringing back meat. She was already prepared for it.

James had been watching her the last part of the trip. When she wasn't on horseback, she was working. She accomplished more than many of the men on the wagon train. Peyjunta cut large pieces of meat and distributed them to some of the other tepees. Anpetu Wi was busy hanging meat above the fire she had started outside. She had built a frame out of branches to hold the meat. She also had a metal pot and was boiling some type of plant.

After that evening's meal, it seemed everyone was happy to be together. There was singing and much conversation. James couldn't understand all of it, but he understood the joy they were experiencing being together in this valley.

Akicita came out of his tepee and walked over to James. He had a small box with him. When he handed it to James, he was shocked to see the trust he was showing. The box contained .45-caliber rounds for his revolver.

James looked him in the face and told him, "Thank you," in both English and Lakota. He put six rounds in his revolver and holstered it. He then put some of the rest in his belt loops. The remaining bullets he left in the box and put the box in the tepee with his blanket.

He sat between Peyjunta and Anpetu Wi. They made small talk and enjoyed each other's company. Peyjunta was learning English quickly, and Anpetu Wi was now showing an interest. They agreed to teach each other. The two of them began learning English as fast as James was learning Lakota.

The seasons passed and then turned in to years. James stayed with them as they moved north to south and south to north with the changing of the seasons. Tonka James was by Peyjunta's side all the time. Peyjunta taught him to hunt, track, make snares and traps, and move silently. They would often leave the others for days to hunt and explore. James felt Peyjunta was like a brother. He had lost one but gained another. James had taught Peyjunta much about the White man's life. And James had become one of the tribe. When traveling and they encountered White men, James was never recognized as being White. Sometimes, he would speak English to them, and they were surprised to learn he was not Lakota. He told them his heart is Lakota. Most White men seemed to resent what they thought was the betrayal of his people.

James had been with the Lakota for seven years and now thought of Peyjunta as a full brother. Peyjunta had taken a woman several years ago and now had two sons. James would sometimes look at Peyjunta's sons and wonder if what he felt was what his Uncle Owen felt when he watched him and Peter grow up. He loved the two boys and thought of them all as his new family. That was not the case with Anpetu Wi. She was now a beautiful woman and very much aware that James noticed her. When others weren't around, she would bump in to him and constantly tease him. She knew she was exciting him and enjoyed it. Most of the other young women were with men, and he knew there were other young men interested in her. It wasn't just her beauty; she was a hard worker, a strong woman, and truly warmed those around her like the sun she was named after. Anpetu Wi had lost her parents in the raid by the cowboys that started all the killing. James and Anpetu Wi had both suffered the same loss and same pain. James was in love with Anpetu Wi. And he knew it wasn't because they both had the same loss. He loved her for who she was and what she made him feel. It would be hard to tell Peyjunta how he felt and that he wanted Anpetu Wi to be his woman and be his family.

CHAPTER 13

A Family Bonded by Love

It was evening, and James was in Peyjunta's tepee sharing a meal. He wanted to get Peyjunta alone to ask permission to have Anpetu Wi. Even though they were like brothers, he wasn't sure how he would respond to James asking for Anpetu Wi. No matter how close the bond had grown, James was a White man. Could he be accepted as a true member of the family?

After eating and James still worrying about how to talk to Peyjunta, his woman got up and brought a present over to James. It was a star quilt. James was caught off guard but knew what it meant. The quilt was given as a gift to a family to be used to warm them and their children. He looked up, and everyone was smiling at him, even the two little children. Anpetu Wi had been sitting next to him all through the meal. James explained his spirit is hungry and thirsty. Only Anpetu Wi can satisfy the hunger and thirst he feels. He received Peyjunta's approval but, most importantly, Wi's. James called her Wi for short, and she was now to be his. He and Wi hugged each other.

Peyjunta and James spoke later. James had nothing to give for Wi, and Peyjunta knew that. Peyjunta didn't always follow customs, and told James his gift to the family was to make his sister happy. He told James the loss of family brought their lives together. Now, together, a new family rises. James promised from his heart and spirit to bring her happiness.

The ceremony was only a few days later. It was late in the afternoon. Men beat drums and played instruments similar to flutes. James had heard them before, but this time, the music was even better. There was much happiness and food. After the ceremony, James and Wi went to his tepee. It was familiar to Wi as she had helped him build it. Before she went in, Wi smiled and said, "Wah gnee ktya" (I am going home).

He told her, "Our home."

She responded, "Our home."

It was a fine tepee. And because of the tribe moving during the seasons, it was easily taken down and put up. As they moved during the seasons, from location to location, they began to meet and communicate with more and more White families. Wi became very fluent in English and more comfortable around White people. Most of the people they had seen were families still moving west or going from one place to another. Many were still frightened at the sight of Indians but soon relaxed as they communicated and realized they were no threat. There were, however, some outbreaks of violence and skirmishes between various groups of Whites, the Army, and some of the other Indian groups. Regardless of the treaties, the White man kept encroaching on the Lakota lands. The future did not look good for the Lakota. On the reservations, they were given food, but not much. And they were no longer allowed to hunt buffalo. The White man's tribes were too many and too big, and the Lakota knew it.

The two years after their marriage went smoothly. In the first year, Wi had a baby girl. James felt if it was possible for anyone to be more beautiful than Wi, it was his daughter. She was born on a beautiful spring morning. As James stepped out of the tepee, everything was covered with dew, the sun was shining, and the air was so fresh. He went back in and told Wi he wanted to call her Chumani (Dewdrops). She was born on a beautiful morning. Chumani was healthy and grew quickly. She was also picking up both languages, Lakota and English. The world was changing, and James and Wi knew she would have to be able to walk in the worlds of both people. Peyjunta would often show up. He seemed to enjoy his visits and spending time with Chumani. Peyjunta had great love for James, Wi, and Chumani.

CHAPTER 14

Everything Changes

James would often go to towns and find work to earn some money for items they didn't need, but were nice to have. He looked half Indian and half White. He wore moccasins and a serape, so some places were reluctant to hire him, even for just simple labor jobs. But he always seemed to manage. When people found out how hard he worked, they would often help him find other small jobs. Each one seemed to lead to another.

On one occasion, he rode into a town wearing his revolver. The serape usually covered it. But this time, as he was getting off his horse, it was exposed. And fortunately so, a business-looking man walking by saw the revolver and made a comment that he had seen one just like it. "Good morning, young man. I couldn't help but notice your Colt. I used to be a salesman for Colt, so I notice guns more than most people probably would. And I've only seen one other revolver nickeled with that same engraving and the handmade ivory grips like yours. They must have been made by the same gunsmith."

James was instantly curious. "Where did you see another gun like this?"

The businessman told him there was a young sheriff in a town called Kearney. He said he was sure the revolver was identical and asked if he could hold it. James pulled the revolver and handed it to the man. He examined it closely and told him he had also held the other. "Yep, it's exactly the same. See the engraved name on the end of the butt strap. Yours says James, his had Peter written on it."

As he handed it back and watched James holster it, he commented that the sheriff's holster was also just like his. They spoke for a few minutes, and the businessman went on his way. James could not believe what he had just heard. He showed no excitement to the businessman, but James knew he had to get the revolver his brother owned. He picked up a few items in town and then left to get back to the village. He couldn't get the revolver out of his mind. Was the sheriff his Uncle Owen, and had he found the revolver next to Peter's body? But the businessman said the sheriff was a young man.

James was puzzled, but he knew he had to go to Kearney to find the revolver.

When James got back to the village, the first thing he did was tell Wi about the revolver. He would have to go to Kearney. She knew the story of the wagon train attack, his brother, and the matching revolvers his uncle had given the two boys. She understood and would go with him. He had been saving some money, so they could function in the White man's world for a short period of time. He would also probably need some money to purchase the revolver. They packed up some essentials, gave their tepee to Peyjunta, explained what they were doing, and left the following morning. They had their horses, and James had traded for two good saddles months earlier. One of the horses pulled a travois behind with Chumani and the items they would need along the way. With the hope of seeing them again, Peyjunta watched them ride off.

Tonka James turned in his saddle and smiled at Peyjunta. "We'll be back, my brother."

Peyjunta knew the word of Tonka James had much honor.

It was summer, so they were farther north than usual. The ride to Kearney took three full weeks. They were lucky as the weather was good all the way. They arrived at the outskirts of Kearney in the late afternoon. Rather than ride into town, they set up a small campsite mostly hidden from view and built a fairly smokeless fire. James hadn't been this far south since he was eleven, and wasn't sure what he was going to encounter. The following morning, he saddled up his horse. He didn't have a hat, and his hair was long. He hoped he wouldn't stand out too much. Even though it was going to be a very warm day, he wore the serape to keep his revolver covered. He rode off, leaving Wi and Chumani at the camp. She had a rifle, and he felt sure she would be safe. She was incredibly strong, clever, and filled with the wisdom of someone much older than her.

He rode into town and was surprised to see how large it was. Most of the towns they had been in were small. He rode up the street and had to ask for directions to the sheriff's office. He rode up in front of one of the stores and tied his horse. He walked over to the sheriff's office, and no one was inside. He started walking, looking in store windows, and just visually exploring the town. He felt comfortable since no one seemed to pay any attention to him. He began to feel more relaxed. He glanced back at the sheriff's office several times. Finally, he saw a young man about his age and size go inside. He turned and went back to the building and entered.

The sheriff was sitting at a table with his head down and writing. He looked up and asked if he could help.

James felt he had just been struck with lightning. He looked at the man for a second and asked, "Who are you?"

The sheriff answered, "I am the sheriff. May I help you?"

James again asked, "I mean, who are you? What's your name?"

The man at the desk answered, "My name is Peter Clark. What is it you need?"

James held out both hands, his whole body was shaking, and said, "I thought you were dead. I saw you get shot and lying on the ground. No one was alive."

Peter asked, "What are you talking about? The last sheriff was shot, but not me."

"No," said James. "Shot on the wagon train, you were shot, and everyone was dead. Uncle Owen had gone for help."

Peter was startled and stood up. "How do you know about any of that?"

James answered, "I am James. I came here because someone told me he had seen a revolver just like mine." He pulled back his serape and showed his revolver.

Peter was even more puzzled; he had always believed James had been killed and was left in one of the wagons. He walked over to James and looked him in the eyes and realized he was looking at himself. They both grabbed each other, stood quiet for a moment, and then stepped back. Peter said, "I always believed you were dead and burnt in one of the wagons. When Uncle Owen got back with help, they found me and Albert. I had been shot and was the only survivor."

James just started blurting things out, "I was the only one standing when the Indians came in. I ran out of ammunition, but didn't run or hide. One of the Indians spoke English and told me I had a strong spirit and they wouldn't kill me. They put the dead in the wagons and set them on fire, but I didn't let them touch you. I remember seeing Albert lying at your side. They took me with them. Over the years, I became one of them, and I'm not sorry for that." The words seemed to just keep pouring out.

Peter said that was okay and told of his recovery from the wound and moving to Kearney. He told the whole story about the Johnson family, his wife Sarah, their son James, and that Uncle Owen lives with them.

The conversation then switched to the present. He told of the shooting of the last sheriff and how Peter took his place. Peter told about Franklin and his men. He said, "It was one of Franklin's men that killed the sheriff, and I know Franklin ordered it, but I was not able to prove it. The sheriff was a good man and taught me much. He is the reason I wanted to be a sheriff."

Peter went on to explain how Franklin is now starting an extortion scheme and explained what that was to James. He explained how Franklin was getting the local businesses to pay a weekly sum to make sure nothing happened to their businesses. In the beginning, one of the businesses told him no. That night, their business caught fire. He told James he was going to send Franklin to jail but needed proof. Peter explained, "I have an obligation to Sheriff Joe and the town of Kearney to make sure Franklin receives justice."

The conversation went on, and James told of Wi and his daughter and how they had given him a good life. Soon they realized they had been talking all afternoon and it was getting late. Peter was excited to take James home and introduce him to Sarah and little James, and for James to see Uncle Owen. He told James that Albert was still alive, and it would be interesting to see if he still remembered him. They got up and started out the door.

CHAPTER 15

Life Shattered Again

As they stepped out on the boardwalk, a shot rang out, and Peter fell back against the wall. Everyone on the street turned and looked. Some came running. James looked across the street where the sound of the shot had come from and saw what appeared to be a small puff of smoke. He looked down at Peter, then ran across the street and in between two buildings. There was a man riding away at full speed. James fired one shot, and the man appeared to jerk on his right side. He was then too far away to waste another shot. He went back to his brother. He was dead. He had died instantly, as the shot hit him directly in the heart. He heard someone was getting the doctor. James felt it was he who had just died. He didn't know what to do or say; he just walked off, got on his horse, and went back to Wi.

When he rode up, Wi could tell something was very wrong. James got off his horse, looked at Wi, and thanked her for being in his life. They sat down, and she gave him something to eat. He explained to her what had just happened. He told her of the pain he felt when he was eleven and left the wagon train. It was not the same; this time it was worse. Wi reminded him of what Akicita had told him—that he had a strong spirit. She said she was sure his brother also had a strong spirit. They both talked for hours. James told her all about when he was small before they got on the wagon train, how he and his brother always played together, how close they were, and how his Uncle Owen had been so important in their lives.

In the conversation, Wi again said, "You and your brother Peter have a strong spirit. You will be well again."

All of a sudden, James had an idea. He told Wi he was going to be Peter's spirit. Wi didn't understand, so James explained, "What if the town saw Peter come back from the dead? While Peter and I were talking to each other, we were both surprised at how much we still look alike. We are the same height and weight. There was a small mirror in the sheriff's office, and we kept looking at how much we looked alike. What if I became Peter's spirit to hunt down whoever killed him?"

Wi wasn't sure how it could be done, but liked the idea. James thought for a time and then told her he would be back. He got on his horse and rode off.

Peter had told James where his house was. James rode to what he thought was the house. It was the middle of the night, but a lamp was on. James walked up on the porch and knocked on the front door. A dog barked, and a man opened the door. James only said, "I am James."

The man got angry and slammed the door. James again knocked. He knocked several times. The dog didn't bark, but he could hear it sniffing at the door. Finally, he said, "Uncle Owen, it's me, James. I was with Peter today. Please open the door."

Uncle Owen opened the door and looked as if he had seen a ghost. Albert didn't bark, but smelled his leg and acted confused. James said he had to speak with him and asked to please let him come in.

A woman came from a back room. She had pain on her face and tears in her eyes. She looked in James's face and had to grab the table to keep from falling.

James again asked, "May I come in?"

Uncle Owen allowed him to come in. Sarah just sat and stared. James starting telling Uncle Owen about coming to town because he heard about a gun like his, and he showed the revolver. He started with seeing Peter in town and how they had spent the whole afternoon talking. He told Uncle Owen about the wagon train, his life, and thinking everyone was dead. He explained, "I was at Peter's side when he was shot. We had just left the office and were on our way here when a shot came from across the street. I ran into the space between the buildings and saw a rider leaving on a horse at full speed. I was only able to get one shot off, but I think I may have hit the man in the right shoulder as he rode off."

Sarah just kept listening. Albert sat by James's leg. James told them why he had come in the dark. He said, "I was told by the Indians I have a strong spirit. My woman told me she was sure Peter did too. I want to be his spirit. I am going to be his ghost and hunt the killer. Do you understand?"

Uncle Owen said, "I'm not sure. Are you saying you're going to make people think you are Peter's ghost?"

James explained, "Peter and I kept looking in the mirror and couldn't believe how much we still looked alike. I plan to cut my hair, dress like Peter, and hunt the man that shot him. I will find him."

Sarah just continued to listen as Uncle Owen and James made plans. They would need to have the doctor's help. Uncle Owen told James that was no problem. He was a good man and a very close friend. They would bury Peter in the backyard, in an unmarked grave, but mark it later. Peter asked if there was any place they could secretly get some dynamite. Uncle Owen told him Johnson's general store had dynamite for blowing up stumps and helping the farmers. He explained Sarah was their daughter and would do anything to help and keep it a secret.

James thought for a minute, then said, "I need you to put some dynamite in the coffin. Sarah, you need to tell everyone at the funeral that Peter told you, if he was shot like Sheriff Joe, he would come back and seek revenge. When you do this, I need you to point to Franklin so I know who he is. After everyone leaves the graveyard, connect the fuse, and cover the hole. Later, when it gets dark, I'll light the fuse. After the explosion, I'll walk out of the graveyard hoping to be seen."

Uncle Owen thought it was a crazy idea, but he had no better one. Peter would be buried tomorrow afternoon. Uncle Owen would have to get the doctor first thing in the morning and explain what was going on. They would put weight in the coffin so no one would be aware it was empty. Uncle Owen and the doctor would fill the grave and make sure the fuse was connected and sticking up out of the ground. They could move Peter's body from the doctor's office to the backyard tomorrow night. James then asked if he could bring Wi and his daughter to stay with them. He didn't want to leave them out there until this was over.

Sarah spoke up, "Please do. I think it would help both of us. Whether she knows it or not, we are now her family too."

Sarah cut James's hair and gave him Peter's clothes and his hat. She was shocked at how much they were the same. She felt she was cutting Peter's hair. James said he would watch the funeral from a distance and see where the fuse was and watch for Sarah to point at Franklin. Then after dark, he would bring Wi and their daughter and go back to the graveyard. Before he left, he told Uncle Owen Peter had told him of a diary. He needed that diary and asked if he could get it from the sheriff's office. James then rode off to tell Wi their plan.

The next day, as James had said, he lay in the grass at a distance and was unnoticed. He watched the funeral and saw Sarah point to the man he had been told by Peter was the problem. He then watched everyone leave. Sarah's parents were the last to leave. They stayed behind and spoke with her and Uncle Owen for a short time and then left. Uncle Owen jumped in the hole and attached the fuse. He uncoiled it until it stuck out of the hole. He and the doctor filled the hole with dirt. It appeared it was only about three to four feet deep, so it didn't take a long time. James rode back to the campsite and got Wi, his daughter, and their personal items. They arrived at Peter and Sara's home after dark. People were still there giving their condolences, so they waited until everyone had left. Then went to the back door and knocked.

Sarah answered; she was obviously still overcome with sorrow but welcomed Wi and James's daughter with a sincere warm heart. James told Uncle Owen and Sarah to stay inside until tomorrow and then to do whatever they would normally do. He then told Wi to have no concern because Uncle Owen would protect them, and he knew Peter had picked a remarkable woman. She would care for them. Little James was still up and was curious about their daughter; the two instantly made friends. Little James was not aware his father was gone, and that was good. James explained his daughter's name, Chumani, which meant dewdrops, and why they named her. Uncle Owen said he didn't care; he was going to call her Sunshine.

Just before walking out the door, James asked for a small amount of flour. Sarah looked puzzled but gave it to him rolled up in a handkerchief. James had put their horses in the stable behind the house. He then left on foot.

CHAPTER 16

The Illusion Begins

It took James about an hour, but he made his way to the graveyard unnoticed by anyone. He had gotten some matches from Uncle Owen, lit the fuse, and got back at a good distance. He then took the flour and patted it all over his face. He hoped it would give him a more convincing look of death. Within a minute, the dynamite went off. The explosion was bigger and made more noise than he had expected. He thought to himself that the doctor and Uncle Owen had gotten a little carried away with the explosives. He was sure the whole town had heard it, but maybe that's what he needed. Before the dust had settled, he started walking toward the town. Some windows were already being lit, and people were looking out. He walked down the main street and straight toward the sheriff's office. People were coming out of the saloon, and James could see the two gunmen he felt Peter was so suspicious of. One had his right arm in a sling. He opened the front door of the sheriff's office, walked into the darkness, then went quickly to the back door, and left.

The two gunmen ran to the front door and started shooting as they entered the building. Both emptied their revolvers. There must have been twenty people in the street watching by now. There was very little light from the moon, and with everyone watching what was going on at the sheriff's office, James was able to slip back across the street in the dark. When the two came out of the sheriff's office, they said no one was there.

One of the men in the crowd was laughing as he said, "You fools, you can't shoot a ghost."

The two gunmen quickly got on their horses and left town. Several of the others including some of Franklin's cowboys returned to the saloon. After James had crossed the street, he went behind the saloon. He was able to see in a rear window and could hear the men inside. He stayed in the shadow, so the light didn't show his face. They were all talking and describing what they had seen and what couldn't possibly be. Several patrons were talking about what Sarah had said at the funeral. Sheriff Peter would be coming back. They were so involved in their conversation that they didn't see or hear James slip in the back door and take a seat behind a table at the rear of the room. He sat there for several minutes, and finally, someone saw him. The men were almost frozen with fear.

James got up, walked to the middle of the room, faced the men, and softly said to Franklin's cowboys, "Tell Franklin I said I would be back." He then slowly walked out the front doors. He quickly slipped around the corner and watched the cowboys come out.

They both looked up and down the street and saw no one. They mounted up and left town as fast as their horses could go.

James slipped out of town and back to Sarah's, went to the stable behind the house, and slept the rest of the night. Just after dawn, he went to the rear door and quietly knocked. He was told to come in; they were already up. Sarah was making something to eat. No one really felt hungry, but it was necessary to eat. Wi was more than anxious to help her. She started the fire on the stove and told Sarah she had never cooked on a stove, only an open fire. James ate and explained what he had done. He told Uncle Owen of the man having his arm in a sling. He wanted him to ask the doctor if he had taken care of anyone with a gunshot wound.

Uncle Owen said, "I'll ask, but if he had, he would already have told us."

They heard voices, and then someone was at the front door. James just nodded and slipped out the back door.

There were several people in front of the house. As soon as Sarah opened the door, they all began talking at the same time. They told

Sarah Peter had come back last night and how many people in town had seen him. They were almost hysterical. They told of how he had walked through town in front of everyone and walked into his office and just disappeared.

One woman was saying, "Sarah, it's true, just like you said. He has come back to find out who shot him." After a pause, she added, "And I'm glad."

Another woman was visually upset and said, "The pastor is telling the townspeople Satan is involved, and revenge is not the work of the Lord."

Sarah interrupted, "I'm sure the Lord believes in justice."

Sarah and Uncle Owen listened, and then told the people they had to go. Sarah explained, she just needed to be left alone. When they left, Sarah looked at Uncle Owen and said, "I think this is working. James may be more like Peter than anyone could have imagined."

Then she looked at Wi and said, "I see why you love him. It's for the same reasons I loved Peter. We are lucky women."

Wi walked over to Sarah and held her for a moment. Although from two different cultures, their hearts were as much alike as Peter and James. Sarah then told her, "I'm glad you're here. I needed you and didn't even know it."

After everyone had left, James came back in. He held his daughter and little James in his lap. Albert seemed to stay at his side the whole time. It was obvious Albert remembered him.

Uncle Owen and James talked and tried to think of what to do next. They didn't come up with any ideas, and James was concerned the two men he was suspicious of would leave the area. He felt sure the man with his arm in a sling was the man he shot riding away. He considered just going out and shooting them both, but that wouldn't solve the problem of Franklin. He had Uncle Owen show him the diary. They went through Peter's notes. James thought the only way they could prove what Franklin was doing was to get the two remaining gunmen to confess. From Peter's notes, it seemed the two came to town on Fridays to collect from the local businesses. He had to scare the truth out of them when they came to town. And tomorrow was Friday.

James asked Uncle Owen to go to the graveyard and fill in the hole before anyone realized what had happened. He asked if he would stay in town for a while and see what other information he could pick up. James said, "While you're gone, I'll try to think of another plan."

Uncle Owen left after eating and went to the graveyard. There was a shovel there, and he used it to fill in the hole from the explosion. He went back to town and did find one of Franklin's men. He asked about the two gunmen Franklin had hired. He was told last night really spooked them, especially the one with the injured arm. He told him about the other cowboys coming back to the ranch from the saloon and that they had seen Peter and were told to tell Mr. Franklin that he said he would be back. The two men told Mr. Franklin they were leaving, and Franklin told them they were doing exactly as they are told. The men were upset but said they would stay.

When Uncle Owen came back to the house, he seemed to enjoy telling James about the two gunmen being spooked. Uncle Owen's face changed; he started showing anger and said, "I want those men to be tortured with fear and then somehow to die a slow and horrible death."

James told him, "Uncle Owen, look at me. I promise they will get their justice. I'll make sure."

In Peter's diary, he had made notes about one of the places Franklin's men went. It was the blacksmith's building. He asked Uncle Owen about the blacksmith.

Uncle Owen told him, "He was the first to help Peter and me when we came to town. He's an honest man and a loyal friend. If you need his help, he will give it to you."

The next morning, James went to the blacksmith and didn't tell him who he was, but did tell him not to be afraid. He asked if Franklin's men had been there yet. He was told no. James told him, "No matter what happens, just pretend I am not here, and you can't see me." He added, "When Franklin's men come, make sure they come all the way in the building."

James stepped into the first stable by the two large front doors and waited what seemed like hours. When the two gunmen showed up, they had three other cowboys with them. James felt the two gunmen had probably been spooked so much; they wanted protection. They had most likely picked three of the toughest cowboys Franklin had.

James hid at the rear of the stall and watched them come in. The blacksmith stayed at the rear, working some metal on the anvil. As the five men walked in, James stepped out behind them. All he said was "Men, don't touch your guns."

All five men turned around and looked shocked. James had put some more flour on his face just for effect.

After a minute, the man with his arm in a sling said, "You can't shoot all of us before we get you."

At that moment, the blacksmith at the rear of the building said, "Who are you men talking to? There is no one there."

James couldn't have asked for better help.

James said, with a slight laugh, "You can't kill a ghost. You didn't do well the other night in my office. I stood right there by the cell and watched you make fools of yourselves. If any one of you pulls a gun, I'll gutshoot all five of you and watch you squirm and scream in pain. I'm sure you've heard what a horrible slow death a gutshot can be."

There was no answer. James asked, "You three cowboys, why are you here?"

All three answered that they had just been told to come.

James then asked, "Do you know what these two are here for?"

Again all three answered and said they didn't know what the two were doing. "We were just told to come."

James laughed. "Well, do you three want to be the first to be gutshot?"

The three just shook their heads. James told them to drop their guns, go out front, get on their horses, and leave. They dropped their belts and left. James could hear the horses ride off. He then asked, "Why are you two here?"

At about the same time, the blacksmith asked again, "Who are you talking to? Aren't you here for Franklin's stolen money?"

The two were on the verge of pure terror. The blacksmith's comment didn't seem to give them any confidence. James was actually enjoying this. He asked again, "Why are you here at the blacksmiths?"

There was a pause, and the one without the sling said they were here to pick up Franklin's money. James asked, "Just what money belongs to Franklin?"

The same gunman said, "If people don't pay Franklin, then we are supposed to burn down their business. Almost every business in town pays us not to burn their business."

James said, "Your truthfulness just saved you from a gutshot." He then asked the man with his arm in the sling, "Why did you shoot me? And before you answer, remember how painful a gutshot is."

He answered, "Franklin told me to. Because you were asking people about the payments they were making for protection."

James said, "You just saved yourself from a gutshot. If you testify to what you just told me, I will try to keep you from being hung for my murder. But you will have to testify against Franklin. Otherwise, you hang for sure."

They both agreed to testify. James had them drop their gun belts and walked them over to the sheriff's office and put them in the cell. The blacksmith had followed them over.

When the cell door was closed and locked, the blacksmith started laughing and asked, "Just who the hell are you?"

James just smiled and said, "An illusion, an illusion of Justice, I now have to get Franklin."

CHAPTER 17

Justice Prevails

James walked over to the telegraph office. The blacksmith was still with him. When he walked in the door, the man inside turned to greet them, saw James, and started to run out the back door.

The blacksmith hollered, "It's okay. Don't be afraid. I don't know who he is, but it's a great day for Kearney."

James wrote on a note that he wanted to be sent to the district judge. The note said, "Peter's murderer arrested—am going after Franklin—he ordered murder also extortion." That was all the message said. From reading Peter's diary, he knew the judge would understand exactly what everything meant.

When the telegraph operator asked who the note was to be from, he said, "James, brother of Peter." Then he turned and walked out of the building.

The blacksmith still at his side stopped him and asked, "Are you really Peter's brother?"

James just looked at him for a moment and then said, "Yes, and I was standing next to him when he was shot. It was the first time I had seen him since we were eleven. We only had a few hours together, and I am going to get Franklin."

The blacksmith told him, "You can't go out to the Franklin ranch by yourself. You really will end up being a ghost. You need to take some people from town with you. Give me an hour, everyone in this town loved your brother, and there will be no problem getting some men together to help you. I'll meet you in front of the sheriff's office in an hour."

James went back to the house and told Uncle Owen and Sarah what had taken place. He told Uncle Owen he was to meet the blacksmith in front of the sheriff's office with several men from the town to arrest Franklin.

Uncle Owen said, "Well, you know I'm going. Let me get my gun and horse."

James said he would meet him in town and left. When James got back in town, he went to the telegraph office again. He told the operator to see what town nearby had a cell he could use for the two prisoners he had in the jail. James thought to himself, *He couldn't put all three men in the same cell because Franklin might get them to change their story.* He told the operator, as soon as he found a town with an empty cell, to ask if the local sheriff could come and transport two prisoners. James wanted to keep Franklin in Kearney where he could watch him.

Men were already gathering at the sheriff's office. The blacksmith had gotten about six, and they were all anxious to see Franklin arrested. They had been told he was James, Peter's brother, so the ghost story had been put to rest. Uncle Owen rode up. James told the men they were going to arrest Franklin for ordering Peter's murder and the extortion of local businesses. They all mounted their horses and rode out of town toward the Franklin ranch.

The three men James had let go at the blacksmith's earlier had gotten to the ranch and told everyone what had happened. They didn't know anything about what had occurred after they left, so they still believed James was Peter's ghost. As the men from town rode up to the ranch, Franklin had his men out front, and he ordered them to open fire. Fortunately, no one from town was hit. Most cowboys weren't the best of shots; that wasn't their profession. James had the townspeople stay just out of range to protect them.

James stood up in the stirrups and hollered to Franklin's men, "I don't want you, men, to die. I am here for Franklin."

He could hear one of the three men he let leave the blacksmith's tell the others, "You can't kill a ghost. He will walk up here and gut-shoot each of us. I'm getting out of here."

Franklin turned and shot him. He told the others, "I'll shoot the next man that tries to leave."

All of the men turned to face him and were pointing their guns at him. One of the men said, "We aren't going to die for you. Drop your gun."

He was furious but did what they said. Then one of the cowboys hollered out they could come get Franklin. The men rode in and could see Franklin being held at gunpoint by several of his men. James got off his horse and walked up to Franklin. Franklin had fear in his face and asked with a trembling voice, "Are you really Peter?"

James answered, "Maybe more than I realized."

Franklin's wife and their older children were now out front. The cowboys told James the family were all good people; it was Mr. Franklin that was the bad apple. Then one of the cowboys turned to Mrs. Franklin and told her they would stay and keep the ranch going. He said they would be proud to remain in her employment. It was obvious she had no love for her husband. She smiled at the cowboys, said thank you, and walked back into the house.

They had the cowboys saddle up a horse for Franklin, and all rode back to town. On the way back, James told Uncle Owen to go by the house. He said, "Let Sarah and Wi know what has happened and that everything is going to be fine. There will be justice."

When they got to town, James asked a few of the men to stay with Franklin. He didn't want him going to jail until he had the two gunmen outside. He then walked over to the telegraph office and asked if he had heard any word. The operator said he had. A sheriff would be here tomorrow to pick up the two prisoners. He added, "The sheriff knew Peter well, and I'm sure he is pleased to take the prisoners and help in any way he can. I've also heard back from the judge, and he'll be here in about three days."

James thanked him for the help and walked out the door. James walked back to the sheriff's office. Franklin and all the men were still out front. James told the men he needed more help. "I am going to put Franklin in the cell, but I need to keep the other two in a separate location. I'll need at least two people to watch them until tomorrow when another sheriff arrives. Can I count on you?"

All six men said they would help. James asked the blacksmith if they could use his place. He simply said, "It would make me proud. Bring them over."

James went into the office and moments later came out with the two gunmen. He told the others to watch them. He then took Franklin in and locked him up. As he came out, the one gunman with his arm in a sling grabbed one of the men's guns from its holster. Before he could even raise it, James fired a shot and got him squarely in the midsection. The man dropped to the ground holding his stomach and squirming. James stepped next to him, holstered his gun, and looked him in the face. "I told you I would gutshoot you. Now you get the death you deserve. I was going to ask the judge to give you life for testifying. Now I don't have to. I thought I was a good person, but I guess not. I'm enjoying watching you suffer, and I hope it hurts real bad!"

The man looked up and said, "You wouldn't let a horse die like this. Can't you finish me?"

James said, "The burning you're feeling is stomach acid, but you're also bleeding out internally, so you'll die soon enough. Too soon to make me happy."

The other gunman watched with bulging eyes. James just told him if he did as he was told, it wouldn't happen to him. The doctor had been called, and the man died just minutes after he arrived. James felt guilty for feeling so pleased.

Several of the men took the other man to the blacksmith's. He was tied and put in one of the stalls. Men took turns watching him until the sheriff came the next day. He brought two extra deputies to use as guards during transport. The sheriff asked about the second prisoner.

One of the men answered, "The one that shot Sheriff Peter died yesterday. The poor guy got gutshot while trying to escape and succumbed to a painful death. It was a sad thing to watch. See how everyone is brokenhearted."

The sheriff looked around, and everyone was smiling. The sheriff said, "I knew Peter well. He was an honorable man and should have lived a long life. I'm pleased to hear of the man's fate, but his justice may have been less than deserved. It's a shame it was so quick."

Two days later, the judge showed up. He met with James and was shocked to see how much the two were alike, not just in looks but also in how they seemed to think and reason. James explained the charges against Franklin. He told of the confession by the two gunmen telling they were ordered to shoot Peter and the extortion of money from local businesses. He also explained the confession was heard by both him and the blacksmith. The gunman that shot Peter was killed in an attempted escape, and the remaining one had agreed to testify against Franklin. The judge was glad to hear they were finally going to get rid of Franklin. He said, "Peter had problems with him for years, and so did Sheriff Joe before him. I'll make sure he gets a fair trial, but I'm sure Franklin had also ordered the killing of Sheriff Joe.

There were two trials. Franklin's was first. His took a full day, and he was found guilty. He was sentenced to life.

The judge said afterward, he felt it would give Franklin more misery than being hung and getting it over with. The second trial was for the last of the three gunmen. He had testified against Franklin as agreed. He was not involved in the shooting of Sheriff Peter. He received a three-year sentence.

None of this brought Peter back. But it was all that could be done. After the trial, James held Sarah and told her he was sorry.

She said, "At least, Peter saw you, and the two of you had time together. Your coming probably gave him the most wonderful gift he could have received. And I don't know if we could have gotten justice without you. Uncle Owen and I are so lucky to have you back and now to have Wi and our special little Sunshine in our lives."

James only answered, "You're the most wonderful gift Peter ever had."

CHAPTER 18

Hearts Begin to Heal

James and Wi stayed a couple of days longer and were able to get to know the Johnsons better and some of the townspeople. Uncle Owen had made a plaque for the wall displaying Peter's nickeled 45. He told James, it would become little James's when he was old enough.

James laughed and said, "Is that when he's about eleven?"

Uncle Owen smiled. "I think that's a good age for a special revolver."

Then all of a sudden his eyes teared up. "I knew two young men that proved that."

James and Wi both felt it was time to go. They had been talking, and wanted to get back to their Lakota family. It was hard for James to explain, but it seemed Uncle Owen and Sarah understood. James told them when the tribe comes farther south next winter, he and Wi and their daughter would come visit. Uncle Owen and Sarah seemed to be satisfied with that. But they did say to make sure they didn't miss a single winter. James agreed. Wi held Sarah for a moment. She kissed her on the cheek and forehead. Then told her in English and Lakota that she loved her like a sister and would miss her greatly.

James then took Sarah to the side and spoke with her alone. "Losing Peter a second time has taken another part of my heart. I know you feel the same. Wi's brother has also become my brother. When I was going through the pain of losing my family he helped me. He told me wounds never go away, but become less painful. Let time heal you, and don't let the wound harden your heart. There are many good men. I know how much Peter loved you, and he would want you to be happy."

Unknown to Uncle Owen and Sarah, James had already saddled the horses and was ready to leave. He couldn't handle a long goodbye. They went out the back door, got on their horses, and rode north.

CHAPTER 19

Home for Summer

The ride back north would be longer. Winter was long over, and the tribe had gone north to follow the game and good weather. James and Wi encountered some rain, but nothing to stop them from getting back to the family. James felt a bond with both cultures but missed Peyjunta and his family. He was looking forward to being home, in his own tepee, and alone with Wi and Chumani. His heart laughed as he thought of calling her Sunshine.

It was another three-week ride, but finally, they came to the last hill before the valley where they knew their people would be. James smiled at Wi as they rode to the top of the hill and looked down on the village. They could smell the fires and food cooking. They noticed their tepee had been set up; they could tell by the paintings on the side. He looked at her and said in Lakota, "Our home."

Many in the village noticed them, and James saw one run to a horse and start up the hill to greet them. As the rider got closer, James realized it was Peyjunta. James felt the pain in his heart was healing.

He really was home. He could only hope Sarah was going to be all right. He knew her pain and how deep it was. He would see her again next winter.

The three of them were welcomed back with great celebration. There were many questions, and Tonka James told them he would have to tell them later. He and Wi were just too happy to be home. After eating and dancing, James, Wi, and Chumani went to their own tepee that Peyjunta had made sure was ready for them. The coldness in his heart from his brother's death was now being overcome by the warmth of love he felt for Wi, Chumani, and the rest of his Lakota family.

Before lying down, James took off his gun belt and removed the revolver. He looked at it for a moment and told Wi, "If a gun could talk, this one would have a hell of a story to tell."

ABOUT THE AUTHOR

Mike Nash is a father of five, a grandfather of seventeen, and a great-grandfather of three and has always loved telling bedtime stories. He has a bachelor's degree in criminal justice and has done everything from farrier work to an investigative position in a law department for a public utility. His hobby is the exhilarating feeling he gets from building hot rods and motorcycles.

CPSIA information can be obtained
at www.ICGtesting.com
Printed in the USA
BVHW032030100323
660178BV00002B/518